TO: Sadie, Our Great-Niece, Christmas 2021

We Love you!
XOXOXO

Love,
Great-Uncle Scott
& Great-Aunt Denise

Fireball Fox
Saves the Forest

WRITTEN & PHOTOGRAPHED BY

Jacqueline Crivello

Acknowledgments

I would like to gratefully thank those involved in the making of this book: Karen McDiarmid for her incredibly blessed vision in the design of these pages; Holly Jorgensen for her unearthly talent in editing skills; Jayme Miner for her courage to help me avoid what I couldn't see; Laurane Lake for her patience with me and amazing web skills. Special thanks to Dan and Renee Crews for sharing their keen eye for wildlife.

Finally, a very special thank you to my photographer mentor and lifetime friend, Peter Read Miller. Without his years of inspiration in my life, this book would not be.

Publisher

Happy Hill Press
P.O. Box 290
Conifer, Colorado 80433
jc@happyhillpress.com
happyhillpress.com

Karen McDiarmid, Book Design
KarenMcDiarmidDesign.com

Crivello, Jacqueline
Fireball Fox Saves the Forest
by Jacqueline Crivello, Evergreen, CO
Happy Hill Press © 2021

Summary: A photographic story of totally awesome Fireball Fox and how he saves the forest from the big rumbling machines. He might have had a little help from some nature-loving humans, but we won't tell him that!

Printed and bound August 2021—#277339
Friesens of Altona, Manitoba, Canada

ISBN 978-0-578-92360-4

Animals; Fox / Birds / Woods / Children
Library of Congress Control Number: 2021942205

10 9 8 7 6 5 4 3 2 1

May God always guide you;
May the angels always keep you;
And may love surprise you
In beautiful and unusual places.

Jacqueline Crivello

Greetings!
I am the spectacular, wonderful
and very magnificent
Fireball Fox.

Are you wondering what makes me
so absolutely awesome?
Well, just wait until you
hear my story!

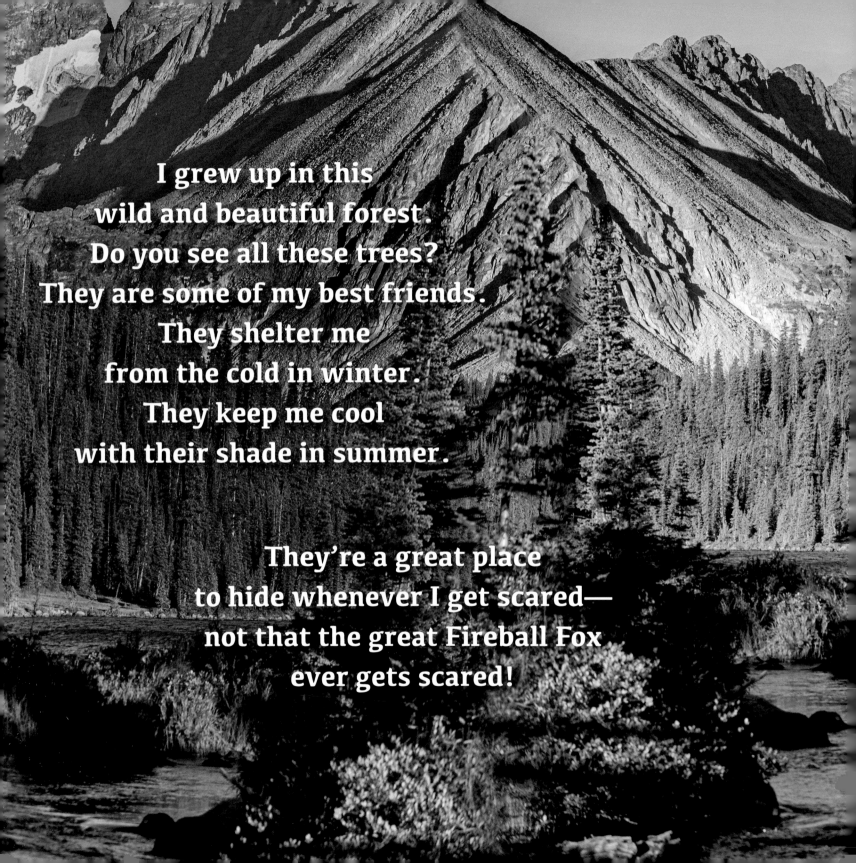

I grew up in this
wild and beautiful forest.
Do you see all these trees?
They are some of my best friends.
They shelter me
from the cold in winter.
They keep me cool
with their shade in summer.

They're a great place
to hide whenever I get scared—
not that the great Fireball Fox
ever gets scared!

Well, okay… maybe just once.
(Actually, this story is all about
that very day.)

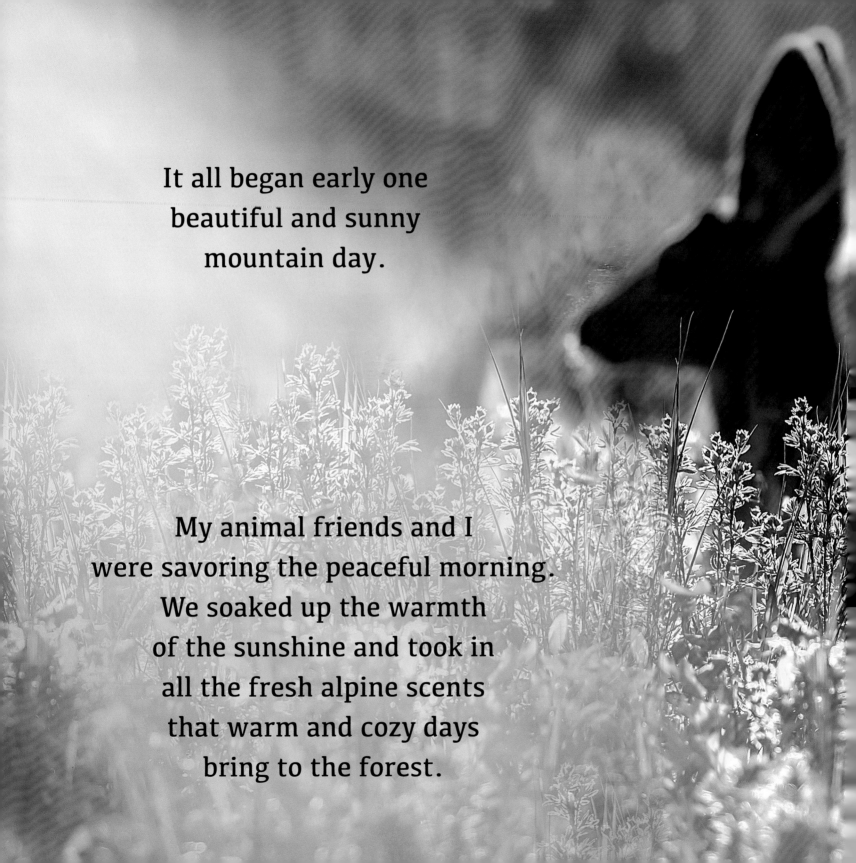

It all began early one
beautiful and sunny
mountain day.

My animal friends and I
were savoring the peaceful morning.
We soaked up the warmth
of the sunshine and took in
all the fresh alpine scents
that warm and cozy days
bring to the forest.

Some were catching up with the neighbors.
Some (like me!) chose to nap
on a cushion of pine needles and evergreen boughs
under the emerald green forest canopy.
The sweet lullaby sound of the nearby stream
calmed me into a gentle sleep.

"Zzzzzzzzzz..."

Even Laythe the mountain lion
took time to nap silently
in the
peaceful breeze.

Everything in the forest
seemed friendly, peaceful
and perfect.

UNTIL...

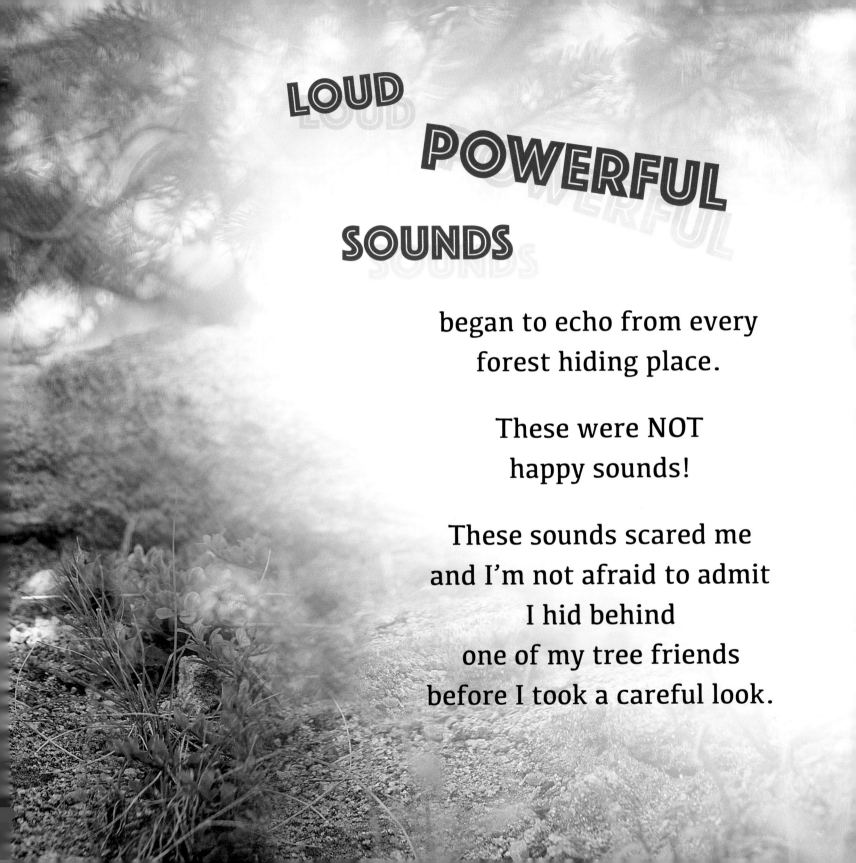

LOUD POWERFUL SOUNDS

began to echo from every
forest hiding place.

These were NOT
happy sounds!

These sounds scared me
and I'm not afraid to admit
I hid behind
one of my tree friends
before I took a careful look.

Even Ernie the elk
was afraid
and hid
behind the biggest rock!

Very big, noisy machines
were cutting down our forest!

"We've got to stop them!"
I cried.

Even the bellowing
of Mort the moose couldn't be
heard over the roar
of the awful machines and
the crash of the falling trees.

"Where will we live if our forest is destroyed? What will we do?" asked Bravo the bobcat.

Chubby Chukar watched sadly
as the machines thundered
through the forest.

"Oh dear!
This is very bad!
Somebody do
something!"
bugled Ernie the elk.

"I can do it! It's me, Fireball!
All my friends are here!
This is our home!
I will save the forest!"

"What will you do, Fireball?"
asked my friend, Finlee Fox.
"Those machines are
big and so terrible!"

"I'm very fast! I'll make them chase me.
They will surely leave when they see me!"
Then, like lightning,
I took off as swiftly as I could run.

The hopeful animals watched as I dodged falling trees, certain I could scare away the mechanical beasts.

But the machines
rumbled on.

I returned, out of breath
but still determined.
"It didn't work! Now what?!" I asked Finlee.

"You can do this, Fireball!"
she encouraged, knowing just how
amazing and awesome I am.

"I know! Make your scariest face.
That will frighten everyone far away.
They will never come back,"
she suggested.

How right Finlee was!
I can look spectacularly scary
when I try.
"I'm going to make myself look
especially terrifying.
That will do it!"

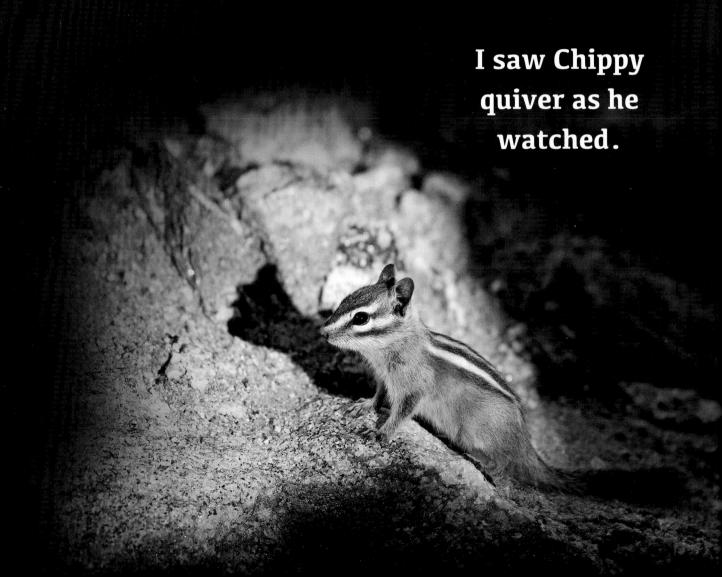

I made such a fierce face
that I almost scared
myself!
I even let out a low growl.

I saw Chippy
quiver as he
watched.

And then...

silence fell over the forest.

I watched in secret
amazement as
the big machines
stopped their work
and began to leave
the forest.

"Fireball did it! He scared them all away!"
the young elk calf exclaimed.

As always, Laythe the lion
was watching all.
"I wouldn't have believed it if I didn't see
it with my own two eyes," he muttered.
"I will never hear the
end of this one!"

The animals weren't the only ones watching.

A boy with a very kind heart and
his wise Grandmother sat at the edge of the forest
as the big, loud machines left
and silence returned.

"The forest is safer from wildfire now,"
Grandmother explained.
"The workers have thinned the trees
to stop wildfire from spreading too quickly.
Young seedlings will grow in their place.
The forest will change, but it will be safer."

"Sometimes it needs our help,
doesn't it, Grandmother?"

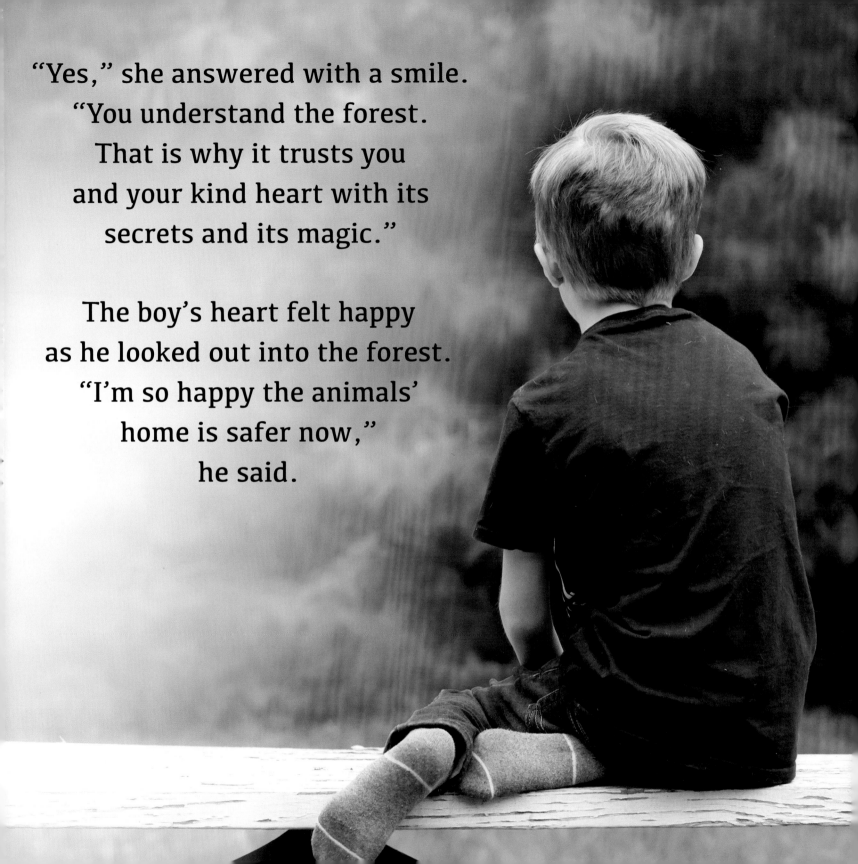

"Yes," she answered with a smile.
"You understand the forest.
That is why it trusts you
and your kind heart with its
secrets and its magic."

The boy's heart felt happy
as he looked out into the forest.
"I'm so happy the animals'
home is safer now,"
he said.

"The machines are gone!
It worked! Fireball, you're a hero!
I knew you could do it!"
Finlee exclaimed.

"Saving the forest
is tiring and
really hard work!"
I yawned.

Then, to the soft sounds
of the whispering wind
and the nearby trickling stream,
I closed my eyes and
drifted back to sleep.